For Sam Sang Seob Bliss

Ronda and David Armitage
When Dad did the washing

PUFFIN BOOKS

This is a picture of the Hubble family.

They live in a house beside the sea.

One morning, Mum had gone to work,

Dad was looking after the children.

"I can't get dressed," yelled Joss, "I haven't got any shorts."
"I can't get dressed," yelled Daisy, "I haven't got any T-shirts."

The washing basket was full, there were no clean clothes to wear.

"Right," said Dad, "let's fill up the washing machine; it's a good day for drying."

In went the T-shirts, the pants and the socks. In went Joss's striped shorts and Mum's new white skirt.

Dad and Amy were answering the front door when Joss remembered his bright red tracksuit.

"That's full enough," said Dad and he shut the washing machine door. Daisy put in the washing powder.

Round and round swished the water.
Round and round swished the dirty clothes.

Soon the washing was finished. Out came the socks, the pants and the T-shirts.

Out came Joss's striped shorts and Mum's new white skirt.
"Oh dear," said Daisy, "a pink T-shirt."
"Oh yuk," said Joss, "pink striped shorts."

"Oh no," groaned Dad, "look at your Mum's new white skirt. It's pink, too. Whatever will she say!"

Joss took out his tracksuit. It wasn't bright red anymore.

"Oh dear," he whispered, "I didn't think."
"I can see that," said Dad.

He stared at the clothes, "Perhaps if we washed everything again the pink would come out."

So they stuffed the clothes back into the washing machine.
Joss held on to his tracksuit.

It was no good, the washing stayed pink. Dad hung it on the line to dry.

All pink and pretty it danced and tugged in the wind.

When Mum came home everyone was very busy.
Dad and Joss were cooking the dinner while Daisy laid the table.
Even Amy was helping.

Mum smiled. "That smells delicious," she said.
And then she saw the pink washing.
"Goodness gracious me, however did this happen?" she asked.

She held up the pink T-shirts, the pink socks and the pink striped shorts.

The pink skirt was right at the bottom of the washing basket.

"My new white skirt," she shrieked, "I've only worn it once."
Nobody said anything. Everyone waited.

"Oh well," she sighed, "I've never had a pink skirt before.
I suppose I'll get to like it in time."

So the next day she wore it to Granny's, with her best striped shirt, and everyone said how lovely she looked.